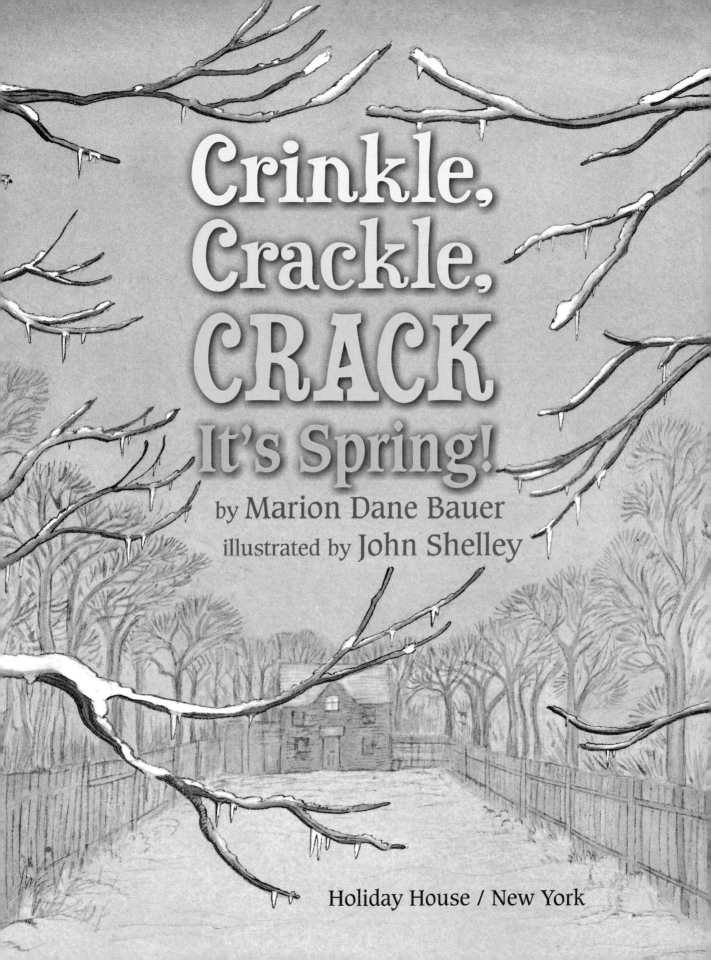

Crinkle, Crackle, CRACK
It's Spring!

by Marion Dane Bauer

illustrated by John Shelley

Holiday House / New York

HOLIDAY HOUSE is registered in the U.S. Patent and Trademark Office.
Printed and Bound in October 2014 at Tien Wah Press,
Johor Bahru, Johor, Malaysia.
The artwork was created with india ink with Leonardt EF Principal Nibs
and watercolors on Arches 300gsm watercolor paper.
www.holidayhouse.com
First Edition
1 3 5 7 9 10 8 6 4 2

Library of Congress Cataloging-in-Publication Data
Bauer, Marion Dane.
Crinkle, crackle, crack : it's spring! / by Marion Dane Bauer ; illustrated by John Shelley.
— First edition.
pages cm
Summary: Invites the reader to join a bear and other woodland animals on a cold,
moonlit walk to investigate strange noises and observe the arrival of spring.
ISBN 978-0-8234-2952-3 (hardcover)
[1. Spring—Fiction. 2. Forest animals—Fiction.]
I. Shelley, John, 1959- illustrator. II. Title.
PZ7.B3262Cri 2015
[E]—dc23
2013012235

For Kathi Appelt,
my picture book guru
—M. D. B.

The illustrations are for Seren
—J. S.

Have you ever awakened
on a late winter night
to a peculiar noise?
Something like
rap, bap, tap,
and then
crunch, scrunch,

followed by

crinkle,

crackle,

CRACK?

If you did,
I'll bet I know what you'd do.
You'd pop out of bed,
you'd creep to the door,
then you'd step outside to see . . .
mud,
rotten snow,
trees shivering in the dark.

And, oh . . . of course,
the bear.
The one standing there
in the middle of your yard.
"It is time," he will say.
"Come with me."

"Time for what?"
you want to ask;
but you hear the sound again,
louder this time.

Rap,
bap,
tap,
crunch,
scrunch,

crinkle, crackle, CRACK!

And you decide to go with the bear.

Hand in paw,
paw in hand,
the two of you set off.
"It is time," sing the buds on the trees.
"It is time," echoes the breeze.
"It is time," hums the bear.
"It is time."

Cold mud sucks at your feet.
The moon is ice.
Even so, traveling with a bear
is rather nice . . .
until you hear,
sniffle, snuffle, snurt!

"What's that?" you cry.
But the bear says only,
"It is time. It is time."

"You're right.
It is time,"
echoes the rabbit,
poking his quivering nose
out of his burrow.
"So I am coming, too."

Rap,
crunch,
CRACK!

"Right there!" you say.
"So close by,"
you say.
"Bear? Do you hear?"
But the bear just lifts
his great head
and calls,
"It is time.
Don't you agree?"

"Cer-cer-certainly,"
the squirrel replies.
"Since it's t-t-time,
may I j-j-join you?"

"It's a pond monster!"
you wail.
But the bear plods on,
silent.

What can you do
but hold tight
to his curving claw
and plod on, too?

"I knew it. I knew it,"
the beaver says,
lumbering after you
and bear and squirrel and rabbit.
"At last! It is time!"

And then,
rap, bap, tap!
Crunch, scrunch!

Crinkle,

crackle,

CRACK!

"Ah," says the bear.
"It is surely time now!"
And the baby bird
pokes his head out and says,
"I hear it is time!
May I come, too?"

And then, there it is.

Rap,
bap,
tap,
crunch,
scrunch,
crinkle,
crackle,
CRACK!

It's spring!

At last!

And you say to the bear,
"I knew it all along!
Didn't you?"